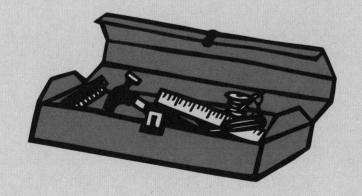

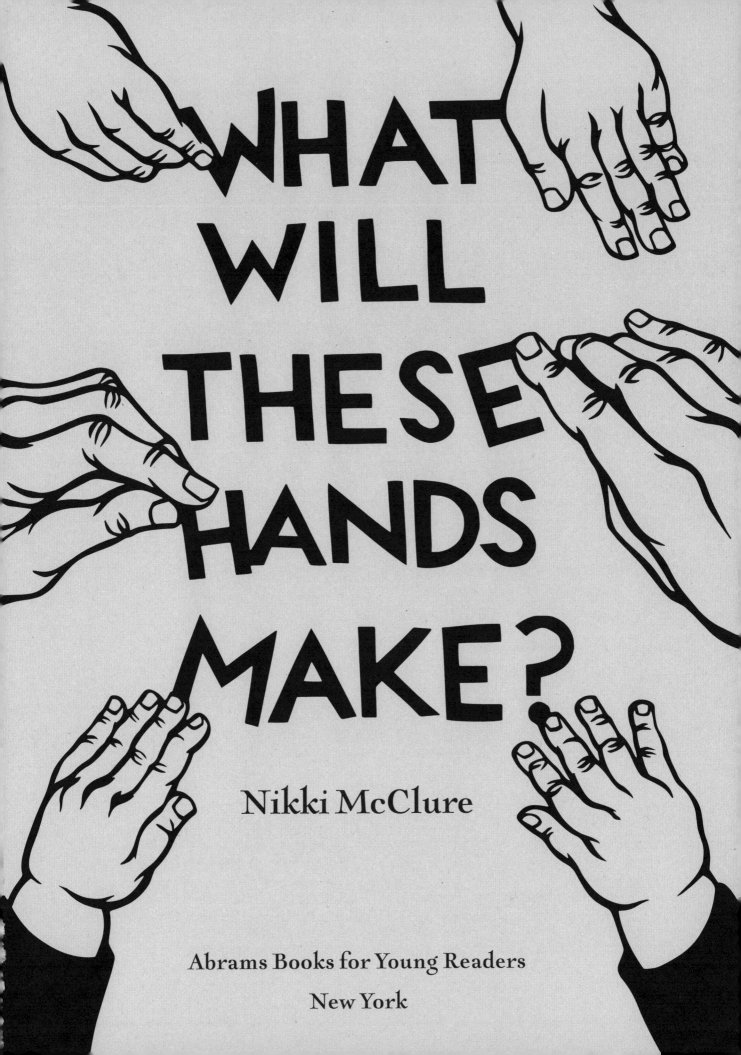

WHAT WILL THESE HANDS MAKE?

Nikki McClure

Abrams Books for Young Readers

New York

FOR FINN AND JAY T.

WHAT WILL THESE HANDS MAKE?

WILL THESE HANDS MAKE:

a teacup for a child

a bowl round and shiny

a quilt to warm

a chair for listening?

WILL THESE HANDS MAKE:

a hat for a baby's head

a wall to walk along

a gate to open

a garden for many?

WILL THESE HANDS MAKE:

a bicycle to ride

a sidewalk safe

a haven for others

a bench to rest awhile?

WILL THESE HANDS MAKE:

a bridge to cross a river

a boat to sail the sea

a house for swallows

a home for families?

WILL THESE
HANDS MAKE:

a sign to point the way
a bouquet to celebrate
a gift to give
a basket for everything?

WILL THESE HANDS MAKE:

a raven from a tree

a cabinet for treasure

a painting bright

a flag to wave hello?

WILL THESE
HANDS MAKE:

a knife to cut carrots

a cake six layers high

a spoon to stir

a song for a parade?

WILL THESE HANDS MAKE:

a pillow for Grandma
a pair of slippers for her feet
a candle to light
a bread to pull apart?

WILL THESE
HANDS MAKE:

a box to hold memories

a bear to sit beside

a book to share

a blanket woven tight?

WILL THESE
HANDS MAKE:

a fiddle to play quick

a stack of wood for the night

a play to cheer

a lantern to guide the way back home?

WILL THESE
HANDS MAKE
A SAFE PLACE
TO BE?

WILL THESE HANDS MAKE A COMMUNITY?

WHAT WILL YOUR

TRACE YOUR HAND HERE

HANDS MAKE?

TRACE YOUR OTHER HAND HERE

AUTHOR'S NOTE

Everything pictured in this book was made by hands, even this book that you are holding. Thank you to the people whose hands helped make this book: the printers, the paper makers, the recyclers, the ink mixers, the boxing-up-the-boxes people, the drivers, the ship builders. We could go on and on, all the way to the bookstore, where hands placed this book on a shelf for you to find.

This book in particular was helped by the hands of Omari, Seya, and Deborah Purce, who modeled for the characters; Scott Ogilvie, my Digital Mage; the makers of my world, Jay T. Scott and Finn McClure; Susan Van Metre, Tamar Brazis, Erica Finkel, Hana Anouk Nakamura, and many hands at Abrams Books for Young Readers; Steven Malk and Writers House; Lois Maffeo; Cynthia at Capitol Florist; Marilyn Frasca; Ira Coyne and Luna; Tibor Breuer; Shanty Slater; Hatcher Cox; Amber Bell; Susanne Wenner; Sophie and Mike Kunka; the sailing vessels *Kirin*, *Scamp*, and *Ichi*; Erik Brown; Alyce Flanagan; Bill Lenker; David Stephens; Eric Fleming; Miriam Klein Stahl; Lena Wolff; Sean, Inger, and Rupert at NW Sails; Sitka canoe carvers; Alexander Forbes; Pete and Annabel Chramiec; Mariella Luz; Calvin Johnson; Tae Won Yu; Roussa Cassel; Julie and Michael Burns; Tove Jansson; Ed Ricketts; Andrea at Browser's Bookshop; Frank and Casey at Danger Room Comics; Jami and Terry at the Sherwood Press; many cake bakers, musicians, sidewalk makers, builders, and cartwheelers; dreamers and makers all.

The images were cut from black paper using an X-Acto blade knife. My left hand held down the paper, while my right hand cut lines and shapes. My hands made what I always wanted to make since I was a child: a book for you.

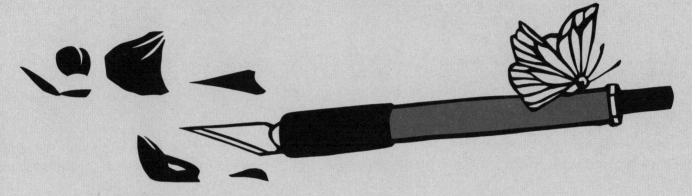

Cataloging-in-Publication Data has been applied for and may be obtained from the Library of Congress.

ISBN 978-1-4197-2576-0

Text and illustrations copyright © 2020 Nikki McClure
Book design by Hana Anouk Nakamura

Printed and bound in U.S.A.
10 9 8 7 6 5 4 3 2 1

Abrams Books for Young Readers are available at special discounts when purchased in quantity for premiums and promotions as well as fundraising or educational use. Special editions can also be created to specification. For details, contact specialsales@abramsbooks.com or the address below.

Abrams® is a registered trademark of Harry N. Abrams, Inc.

ABRAMS The Art of Books
195 Broadway, New York, NY 10007
abramsbooks.com